On with the Circus!

By John McInnes

Drawings by William Hutchinson

GARRARD PUBLISHING COMPANY
CHAMPAIGN, ILLINOIS

Copyright © 1973 by John McInnes   All rights reserved. Manufactured in the U.S.A.
International Standard Book Number: 8116–6722–7   Library of Congress Catalog Card Number: 72–5283

On with the Circus!

Judy Peters walked
into the circus tent.
She climbed to a seat
high above the center ring.
Judy came often,
for her parents
were famous circus stars.

The show began!
First came the lions.
The lion tamer
cracked his whip.
The lions ran around
in a circle.

Then they climbed
on wooden boxes.
The lion tamer
bowed to the people.
He gave Judy
a big smile.

Trained seals came next.
Some did tricks
in a pool of water.
One big seal
held two balls
on his nose
at the same time.
Other seals played music
on toy horns.
The trainer of the seals
gave each a big fish.
Judy liked the seals,
but she could not wait
for the next act.

Her mother and father
galloped into the ring.
Then they rode
standing up on their horses.
"I can do that,"
Judy thought,
"but I'm not old enough."

Then her parents jumped
from one horse to another
as the horses
galloped around the ring.
Finally both horses
danced to the music
of the circus band.

Judy wondered
when she'd be old enough
to perform in the circus.
Next came the clowns
led by a funny band.

Bingo, the smallest clown,
had on clothes
too big for him.
His hat fell down
over his eyes.
He rode around the ring
on the back
of a little pony.

Suddenly the pony stopped,
and Bingo fell off.
He looked surprised.
All the people laughed
and clapped their hands.

Then Bobo, a big clown,
drove a little green car
into the spotlight.
He climbed out
holding a little dog.
Soon eight more dogs
jumped out of the car.

Bobo and Bingo
got down on their knees.
Two dogs jumped
on Bobo's back.
Two dogs jumped
on Bingo's back.
Four more dogs
jumped on top
of the other dogs.
The smallest dog
climbed to the top.
He sat up
on his back legs
and barked.

The clowns and the dogs
did more tricks.
Then Bobo and Bingo
got into the car.
It wouldn't go.
They got out of the car.

The dogs got in.
Bobo and Bingo
pushed the car
out of the ring.
Everyone laughed.
They clapped and clapped.

One afternoon
later that week,
Judy was walking
toward the tent.
She met Bobo,
the tall clown.
He looked very sad.
"Hello, Bobo," said Judy.
"You look sad.
What's the matter?"
"Bingo is sick,
and he can't act
in the show today,"
answered Bobo.

"There's no one here
to take his place."
"There must be someone,"
said Judy.
"One of your friends
could do his act."

"All my friends
are too big," said Bobo.
"I need someone
small enough
to ride Bingo's pony."
"I can do that,"
said Judy.

"I'll help you
with your act."
"Do you really think
you could take
Bingo's place?"
asked Bobo.
"Yes," answered Judy.

"Then we'll change
the act a bit,"
said Bobo.
"I don't want you
to do Bingo's fall
off the pony.
You might get hurt."
"After the act is over,"
Bobo said,
"I'll drive the car
with the dogs
out of the ring.
You ride out
on the pony."

Judy was very excited.
"I'll get ready,"
she said to Bobo.
Judy got dressed
in Bingo's clothes.

Bobo helped her
put on makeup.
He put white paint
all over her face.
He put a green spot
on her nose
and a black spot
under each eye.
Then he gave her
a big red mouth
that went from ear to ear.
"Take a look, Judy,"
said Bobo
when he had finished.

"You look
just like a clown."
Judy looked at herself
and began to laugh.

"No one will know
I'm Judy Peters,"
she said.
Soon it was time
for Judy and Bobo
to go into the ring.

Judy rode in
on Bingo's pony.
The pony galloped
around the ring
and stopped suddenly.
Judy waved to the people.

Nobody laughed.
Judy was afraid
she wouldn't be
a good clown.
Then Bobo came out,
driving the little car.

One by one,
all the dogs jumped out.
They barked
as they danced
around Bobo and Judy.

The two clowns
did all their tricks.
Judy's were so funny
even Bobo laughed at her.

All the people
clapped and clapped.
Now Judy felt better.
Near the ring,
Mr. and Mrs. Peters
were watching the act.

The lion tamer
was watching too.
"Where is Judy?"
he asked.
"I don't see her
in the stands."

"She was coming
to the show this afternoon,"
Mrs. Peters said.
Just then the act was over.
The two clowns
took a bow.

Bobo drove the car
out of the ring.
Judy rode the pony
behind the car.

She stood up
on its back.
The people clapped.
"Who is that
funny little clown
coming out of the ring
on Bingo's pony?"
asked Mrs. Peters.
"It can't be Bingo.
He's sick today."
"I don't know,"
said the lion tamer.
The people
kept on clapping.

Just then
Judy fell off the pony.
"Look! It's Judy!"
shouted the lion tamer.
"The clown is Judy!"
Judy's father ran to her.

"Are you all right?"
he asked.
"I'm all right, dad,"
she said.
"You were a good clown,"
said Judy's mother.

"It was fun
to do Bingo's act,"
said Judy.
"I'm glad I didn't
have to wait
until I grow up
to be in the show!"